A NORTH-SOUTH PAPERBACK

Critical praise for

Spiny

"The chapters in this . . . book are brief, the style is simple and direct, and the plot is filled with action. These attributes, coupled with Uli Waas' soft, delicate watercolors, make this a fine first chapter book; but the warm, affectionate tone and emphasis on security may make it an even better read-aloud for young children. Sweet, in the best sense of the word." *Booklist*

SPINY

BY JÜRGEN LASSIG
ILLUSTRATED BY
ULI WAAS

TRANSLATED BY
J. ALISON JAMES

NORTH-SOUTH BOOKS
NEW YORK / LONDON

Copyright © 1995 by Nord-Süd Verlag AG, Gossau Zürich, Switzerland. First published in Switzerland under the title *Keine Spur von Spino-Dino*. English translation copyright © 1995 by North-South Books Inc.
All rights reserved. No part of this book may be reproduced or utilized in any form or by any means, electronic or mechanical, including photocopying, recording, or any information storage and retrieval system, without permission in writing from the publisher.

Published in the United States, Great Britain, Canada, Australia, and New Zealand in 1995 by North-South Books, an imprint of Nord-Süd Verlag AG, Gossau Zürich, Switzerland. First paperback edition published in 1996. Distributed in the United States by North-South Books Inc., New York.

Library of Congress Cataloging-in-Publication Data is available.
A CIP catalogue record for this book is available from The British Library.

ISBN 1-55858-401-3 (TRADE BINDING) 10 9 8 7 6 5 4 3 2 1
ISBN 1-55858-402-1 (LIBRARY BINDING) 10 9 8 7 6 5 4 3 2 1
ISBN 1-55858-552-4 (PAPERBACK) 10 9 8 7 6 5 4 3 2 1
Printed in Belgium

CONTENTS

Spiny Squeaks Out

A long, long time ago (65 million years ago, to be exact) a little egg started to crack. The egg was in a nest with twenty-three other eggs, and inside each one was a tiny spinosaurus. When the first egg split open, the baby spinosaurus jumped out of the shell and stretched his spiky dorsal fin in the warm sun. He was hungry, so he opened his mouth and started to howl. But he was so small, it sounded like this: "Squeak!"

That tiny noise was enough to bring his mother and father running. A young iguanodon came running too. She wanted to see the new baby. Spiny looked up into the giant friendly faces and knew at once he had found his parents. "I'm hungry," he squeaked. Mother and Father Spinosaurus blinked, shook themselves, and went into action.

"Oh yes, oh yes," Father Spinosaurus said.

"Food for my baby," cried Mother Spinosaurus.

They headed off into the woods.

"Wait!" cried Igu, the iguanodon. "Are you going to leave him here all alone?"

"Keep an eye on him, will you?" Father Spinosaurus called back over his shoulder.

"Don't let him get out of the nest," said Mother.

Spiny felt awful. He had just met his parents, and already they were gone.

"I want my mother!" he wailed. "I want my father."

"Hush hush," said Igu, trying to console him. But Spiny would not stop crying.

"I'll go and find them," said Igu. "You stay right here."

Spiny did not want to stay right there. He wanted to find his parents himself.

As soon as Igu was out of sight, he crawled over the other eggs and slid down the side of the nest.

Spiny Gets Lost

Tall grasses waved in the hot wind. Spiny was thirsty. Suddenly three bright dragonflies hummed past. Spiny ran after them. He was looking up at the dragonflies, and didn't notice the lake. He glanced down just in time and saw another little dinosaur. "Hello!" he said.

The lake didn't answer.

Spiny leaned forward to nudge the other dinosaur in the nose, and *splash*, he fell into the lake. He swallowed a mouthful of water. It was delicious. He tried a lily pad. It was sweet and tender. Spiny played in the lake for a long time.

When the warm sun disappeared behind
dark clouds, Spiny grew cold and afraid.
Where was his mother? Where was his
father? Where was his nest? He had no
idea. He was lost.

The clouds rumbled and shook. Rain
tumbled out in torrents. Spiny looked for
a place to hide.

A Flash in the Dark

Igu didn't find Spiny's parents, and she couldn't find Spiny, either. He was gone!

Suddenly there was a zap of lightning with thunder right behind. The sky opened up and rain poured down. Igu raced for cover in the woods.

Lightning flashed again. In that instant, Igu saw what no dinosaur wants to see: TyRoar, the great tyrannosaurus rex.

An iguanodon can run fast when it is afraid, and Igu ran faster than the rain.

She ran so fast, she almost bumped into her triceratops friend, Topsy.

"Slow down, slow down," Topsy said with her mouth full. "What's the trouble?"

"I saw T-Ty-TyRoar, and I lost the baby spino-spinosaurus, and I couldn't find his parents, and the nest was empty except for the other eggs, and . . ."

"What was that first part?" asked Topsy.

"I saw the tyrannosaurus rex."

"But did he see you? That's the important question." Topsy was always sensible.

"I don't know. I ran as fast as I could."

"And that's fast," Topsy said, smiling. "We're probably safe. For the time being, anyway. Now what's this about a baby spinosaurus?"

Igu told her the whole story, in order this time.

Topsy said, "I'm sure Spiny has been found by his parents by now. No baby would be left alone out in a storm like this. Especially not with TyRoar in the area."

Comforted, Igu curled up next to her friend Topsy and they went to sleep.

Slowly the rain let up, and the smell of magnolias drifted through their dreams.

THE LAKE MONSTER

The next morning the sun was out and the earth was steaming. Topsy and Igu went down to the river to cool off. Just as they stepped in the water, a great spiny fin burst through the surface.

"Yikes!" cried Igu. Topsy stepped back and lowered her horns. But it was only Mother Spinosaurus.

"Good morning!" said Igu cheerfully.

Mother Spinosaurus did not look happy.

"Where is my baby?" she cried.

"Oh-oh," said Topsy.

Igu thought about the storm and TyRoar on the loose, and her shoulders crumpled in shame. "I went to look for you," she said in a small voice, "and when I got back, he was gone."

Mother Spinosaurus started to wail. "I've been up all night, worried. Where could he be? What can we do?"

"Igu and I will look for him right now," said Topsy. "We'll ask everyone we see."

NEVER TRUST A STRUTHIOMIMUS

Just then along came a struthiomimus.

"Mr. Struths," cried Topsy.

"Don't ask him!" said Igu. "He eats eggs!" But it was too late.

"Yes, my dears. How may I help you?"

"It is the new baby spinosaurus," said Igu. "He hatched early, and wandered off and TyRoar is on the loose."

Mr. Struths said, "I see. He hatched early, did he? This is a grave situation. I recommend that we retrace his steps. Show me the nest!"

They marched back to the nest, which was hidden in the ferns.

"Yes, yes," said Mr. Struths, rubbing his forepaws together. "What a treasure, buried treasure. Well, we've found what we were looking for, haven't we?"

"But Spiny is already hatched," said Igu.

"Right. You're absolutely right. I'd quite forgotten. Already hatched. Not nearly so good that way. No, not so fresh."

"So how do we find him?" asked Topsy. She was getting impatient.

"Follow his tracks, of course. Follow his tracks," said Mr. Struths. "They will lead you right to him."

And there, in the mud, were tracks leading down the side of the nest and into the woods. Topsy and Igu set off following the footprints.

As soon as they were out of sight, Mr. Struths snatched an egg and ran off.

Rampho Has an Idea

"Hey hey hey! Where are you two young ones headed, with your noses on the ground and your tails in the air?" It was Rampho, the rhamphorhynchus.

Igu explained everything.

"Come to think of it, I saw a little spinosaurus yesterday. Yes sir, that I did. You see a lot, swirling around in the sky."

"Oh, could you look again?" asked Igu.

"It would be so much faster," said Topsy.

"Lucky for you, I love love love to fly. Take a look at this." Rampho swooped down from the branch and almost brushed the ground, before taking off into the sky.

"Meet me in the field!" he called back.

Away he sailed, circling higher
and higher, and then . . .

down, down, down he plunged, his wings
folded back. He was heading straight for
the ground, faster and faster, but just
before he crashed, he opened his wide

36

wings, swooped up in a little arc, and
landed, light as a feather, on the sand.

"What did you see?" asked Topsy.

"I saw him all right," said Rampho, a
little out of breath. "He's in the woods, by
the gum-gum tree. But I saw something
else, too." He drew in his wings and
snapped his sharp teeth. "I saw the
tyrannosaurus rex."

"TyRoar?" asked Igu,
terrified.

"The beast himself."

LOST AND FOUND

When Spiny woke up that morning, he was confused. This was his second day out of the egg, and he had no idea where he was. Humming insects hovered in the morning mist that rose from the damp jungle floor. Shadows of ferns made stripes across the moss. Where was his warm brown nest, with his brothers and sisters curled up in their eggs beside him?

Where was his mother? Where was his father? He gulped. Loneliness welled up in him and he started to cry.

Curious, other dinosaurs and mammals peered around trees to see who was making the funny noise. But Spiny was so lonely, he did not notice their kind looks.

At last, Mama Mia approached him. She was a maiasaurus, and very gentle with young ones.

"What's wrong, little spinosaur?" she asked. "Are you hungry?"

Spiny was so hungry, he just cried louder.

Mama Mia picked some tender ferns and offered them to the baby dinosaur. He chomped them down.

When he was full, she asked him, "Where are your mother and father?"

Spiny's lip began to tremble again.

But before he could begin to cry, a loud sound came through the woods:

WRUMM! THRUMM! Heavy footsteps shook the ground.

CRASH! CRACK! Tree limbs split like twigs. The noise came closer and closer.

"Run for your lives!" shouted Mama Mia. "It's TyRoar!"

All the dinosaurs scattered.

WRUMM! THRUMM! CRASH!

Spiny turned round and round. He didn't know where to go!

Then he saw a patch of light, and quick as he could, he ran towards it.

"No! Not that way!" cried Mama Mia.

Too late.

TyRoar broke through the undergrowth with a snarl. He saw Spiny and stopped short. Just when he was going to grab the baby spinosaurus and eat him for a little snack, Spiny smiled up at him sweetly.

"Have you seen my father?" he asked.

"WHAR WHROAR WHAT?"

"I can't find my father or my mother," Spiny said. "You're so big and strong, I thought you might have seen them."

"RRI'LL TELL YOU WHAT," TyRoar growled. "COME WITH RRME, AND WE'LL RRSEE IF WE CAN HUMYUM FIND RRTHEM."

So TyRoar snatched Spiny in his claws and ran off.

Meanwhile, Igu and Topsy were following Rampho to the place in the woods where he had seen Spiny. Topsy had her horns sharpened and was raring for a good fight with TyRoar. Igu was so afraid, her legs didn't want to move.

"How about if I go and find Mother and Father Spinosaurus?" she offered.

"Don't be scared," said Topsy. "There are three of us, and only one of him."

They could already hear TyRoar
growling and stomping and cracking
through the trees up ahead. Then they saw
him, huge and dangerous.

And to make matters worse, tiny Spiny was clutched in his claws.

TyRoar flattened everything in his path.

Topsy lowered her horns.

Igu was so angry to see the little spinosaurus helpless in the claws of TyRoar that her heart pounded like thunder.

She took a deep breath and shouted: "IF YOU SO MUCH AS HURT ONE LITTLE SPINE ON HIM, YOU'LL HAVE ME TO DEAL WITH!"

"HRUMPH! WHA . . . ?" TyRoar was so surprised that he dropped Spiny.

That was his big mistake. Topsy charged at him with her sharp horns, and just as TyRoar spun around to swat her, Igu bumped his hind leg and tripped him. He fell sprawling to the ground.

While TyRoar was kicking his legs around trying to stand up, Topsy tossed Spiny through the air to Igu. She caught the little spinosaurus and ran as fast as she could back to the nest.

And iguanodons can run fast!

What a surprise when they arrived at the nest. Spiny had twenty-two brothers and sisters to play with!

Spiny never lost his taste for exploring.
He scrambled up trees to get a good look
at the butterflies. "Look at me," he cried.
"I can fly!" But he just plopped to the
ground.

Igu said, "He may be silly, but he is
brave."

Topsy turned to her friend and smiled.
"Not as brave as you are."

When Mr. Struths heard how brave the others had been, he felt guilty and returned the egg he had stolen to the nest. Mother and Father Spinosaurus were so grateful that when the egg finally hatched, they named the baby, their twenty-fourth, Little Struths.

About the Author

JÜRGEN LASSIG was born in Dresden, Germany. He studied languages and graphic design in Hamburg and in Copenhagen. After receiving his graphics degree, he worked as a printer, and since 1978 he has worked in the publishing business. He has translated several children's books and today is a children's book editor.

Jurgen Lassig lives with his wife in northern Germany, near Hamburg, where his dog often digs in the grass, perhaps hoping to find the tracks of a spinosaurus.

About the Illustrator

ULI WAAS was born in Donauworth, Germany. She studied painting and graphic arts at the Academy of Fine Arts in Munich. She likes to illustrate children's books with animals as the main characters.

Uli lives with her husband, their daughter and son, and a Jack Russell terrier on the edge of the Swabian Alps, where one can still find quite a few fossils.

Uli Waas has also written and illustrated *Where's Molly*, published by North-South.

About the Translator

J. ALISON JAMES was born in
southern California, but she has lived all over
the world. She received a degree in English and
languages from Vassar College, and a master's
degree from The Center for the Study of Children's
Literature in Boston. Since 1985 she has been
writing novels and picture books, and translating
children's books from German and Swedish.

She lives with her husband and daughter in
northern Vermont, where a dinosaur descendent,
nicknamed Champ, is said to lurk in the depths of
Lake Champlain.